TOOTLE

Story by
GERTRUDE CRAMPTON

Pictures by
TIBOR GERGELY

A GOLDEN BOOK • NEW YORK

Copyright © 1945, renewed 1973 by Random House, Inc. All rights reserved. Published in the United States by Golden Books, an imprint of Random House Children's Books, a division of Random House, Inc., New York. Originally published in 1945 by Simon and Schuster, Inc., and Artists and Writers Guild, Inc. GOLDEN BOOKS, A GOLDEN BOOK, A LITTLE GOLDEN BOOK, the G colophon, and the distinctive gold spine are registered trademarks of Random House, Inc. A Little Golden Book Classic is a trademark of Random House, Inc. Tootle is a trademark of Random House, Inc.
www.goldenbooks.com
www.randomhouse.com/kids
Educators and librarians, for a variety of teaching tools, visit us at www.randomhouse.com/teachers
Library of Congress Control Number: 2007922142
ISBN: 978-0-307-02097-0
Printed in the United States of America
40 39 38 37 36 35 34 33 32 31

FAR, FAR to the west of everywhere is the village of Lower Trainswitch. All the baby locomotives go there to learn to be big locomotives. The young locomotives steam up and down the tracks, trying to call out the long, sad *ToooOoooot* of the big locomotives. But the best they can do is a gay little *Tootle*.

Lower Trainswitch has a fine school for engines. There are lessons in Whistle Blowing, Stopping for a Red Flag Waving, Puffing Loudly When Starting, Coming Around Curves Safely, Screeching When Stopping, and Clicking and Clacking Over the Rails.

Of all the things that are taught in the Lower Trainswitch School for Locomotives, the most important is, of course, Staying on the Rails No Matter What.

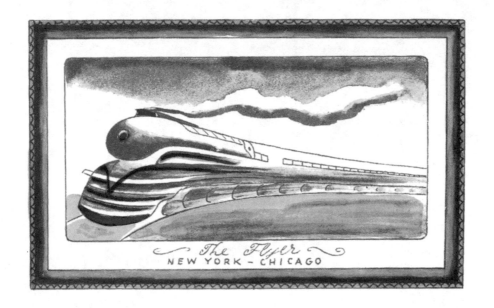

The Flyer
NEW YORK – CHICAGO

The head of the school is an old engineer named Bill. Bill always tells the new locomotives that he will not be angry if they sometimes spill the soup pulling the diner, or if they turn the milk to butter now and then. But they will never, never be good trains unless they get 100 A+ in Staying on the Rails No Matter What. All the baby engines work very hard to get 100 A+ in Staying on the Rails. After a few weeks not one of the engines in the Lower Trainswitch School for Trains would even think of getting off the rails, no matter—well, no matter what.

One day a new locomotive named Tootle came to school.

"Here is the finest baby I've seen since old 600," thought Bill. He patted the gleaming young locomotive and said, "How would you like to grow up to be the Flyer between New York and Chicago?"

"If a Flyer goes very fast, I should like to be one," Tootle answered. "I love to go fast. Watch me."

He raced all around the roundhouse.

"Good! Good!" said Bill. "You must study Whistle Blowing, Puffing Loudly When Starting, Stopping for a Red Flag Waving, and Pulling the Diner without Spilling the Soup.

"But most of all you must study Staying on the Rails No Matter What. Remember, you can't be a Flyer unless you get 100 A+ in Staying on the Rails."

Tootle promised that he would remember and that he would work very hard.

He did, too.

He even worked hard at Stopping for a Red Flag Waving. Tootle did not like those lessons at all. There is nothing a locomotive hates more than stopping.

But Bill said that no locomotive ever, ever kept going when he saw a red flag waving.

One day, while Tootle was practicing for his lesson in Staying on the Rails No Matter What, a dreadful thing happened.

He looked across the meadow he was running through and saw a fine, strong black horse.

"Race you to the river," shouted the black horse, and kicked up his heels.

Away went the horse. His black tail streamed out behind him, and his mane tossed in the wind. Oh, how he could run!

"Here I go," said Tootle to himself.

"If I am going to be a Flyer, I can't let a horse beat me," he puffed. "Everyone at school will laugh at me."

His wheels turned so fast that they were silver streaks. The cars lurched and bumped together. And just as Tootle was sure he could win, the tracks made a great curve.

"Oh, Whistle!" cried Tootle. "That horse will beat me now. He'll run straight while I take the Great Curve."

Then the Dreadful Thing happened. After all that Bill had said about Staying on the Rails No Matter What, Tootle jumped off the tracks and raced alongside the black horse!

The race ended in a tie. Both Tootle and the black horse were happy. They stood on the bank of the river and talked.

"It's nice here in the meadow," Tootle said.

When Tootle got back to school, he said nothing about leaving the rails. But he thought about it that night in the roundhouse.

"Tomorrow I will work hard," decided Tootle. "I will not even think of leaving the rails, no matter what."

And he did work hard. He practiced tootling so much that the Mayor Himself ran up the hill, his green coattails flapping, and said that everyone in the village had a headache and would he please stop TOOTLING.

So Tootle was sent to practice Staying on the Rails No Matter What.

As he came to the Great Curve, Tootle looked across the meadow. It was full of buttercups.

"It's like a big yellow carpet. How I should like to play in them and hold one under my searchlight to see if I like butter!" thought Tootle. "But no, I am going to be a Flyer and I must practice Staying on the Rails No Matter What!"

Tootle clicked and clacked around the Great Curve. His wheels began to say over and over again, "Do you like butter? Do you?"

"I don't know," said Tootle crossly. "But I'm going to find out."

He stopped much faster than any good Flyer ever does, unless he is stopping for a Red Flag Waving. He hopped off the tracks and bumped along the meadow to the yellow buttercups.

"What fun!" said Tootle.

And he danced around and around and held one of the buttercups under his searchlight.

"I do like butter!" cried Tootle. "I do!"

At last the sun began to go down, and it was time to hurry to the roundhouse.

That evening while the Chief Oiler was playing checkers with old Bill, he said, "It's queer. It's very queer, but I found grass between Tootle's front wheels today."

"Hmm," said Bill. "There must be grass growing on the tracks."

"Not on our tracks," said the Day Watchman, who spent his days watching the tracks and his nights watching Bill and the Chief Oiler play checkers.

Bill's face was stern. "Tootle knows he must get 100 A+ in Staying on the Rails No Matter What, if he is going to be a Flyer."

Next day Tootle played all day in the meadow. He watched a green frog and he made a daisy chain. He found a rain barrel, and he said softly, "Toot!" "TOOT!" shouted the barrel. "Why, I sound like a Flyer already!" cried Tootle.

That night the First Assistant Oiler said he had found a daisy in Tootle's bell. The day after that, the Second Assistant Oiler said that he had found hollyhock flowers floating in Tootle's eight bowls of soup.

And then the Mayor Himself said that he had seen Tootle chasing butterflies in the meadow. The Mayor Himself said that Tootle had looked very silly, too.

Early one morning Bill had a long, long talk with the Mayor Himself.

When the Mayor Himself left the Lower Trainswitch School for Locomotives, he laughed all the way to the village.

"Bill's plan will surely put Tootle back on the track," he chuckled.

Bill ran from one store to the next, buying ten yards of this and twenty yards of that and all you have of the other. The Chief Oiler and the First, Second, and Third Assistant Oilers were hammering and sawing instead of oiling and polishing. And Tootle? Well, Tootle was in the meadow watching the butterflies flying and wishing he could dip and soar as they did.

Not a store in Lower Trainswitch was open the next day and not a person was at home. By the time the sun came up, every villager was hiding in the meadow along the tracks. And each of them had a red flag. It had taken all the red goods in Lower Trainswitch, and hard work by the Oilers, but there was a red flag for everyone.

Soon Tootle came tootling happily down the tracks. When he came to the meadow, he hopped off the tracks and rolled along the grass. Just as he was thinking what a beautiful day it was, a red flag poked up from the grass and waved hard. Tootle stopped, for every locomotive knows he must Stop for a Red Flag Waving.

"I'll go another way," said Tootle.

He turned to the left, and up came another waving red flag, this time from the middle of the buttercups.

When he went to the right, there was another red flag waving.

There were red flags waving from the buttercups, in the daisies, under the trees, near the bluebirds' nest, and even one behind the rain barrel. And, of course, Tootle had to stop for each one, for a locomotive must always Stop for a Red Flag Waving.

"Red flags," muttered Tootle. "This meadow is full of red flags. How can I have any fun?

"Whenever I start, I have to stop. Why did I think this meadow was such a fine place? Why don't I ever see a green flag?"

Just as the tears were ready to slide out of his boiler, Tootle happened to look back over his coal car. On the tracks stood Bill, and in his hand was a big green flag. "Oh!" said Tootle.

He puffed up to Bill and stopped.

"This is the place for me," said Tootle. "There is nothing but red flags for locomotives that get off their tracks."

"Hurray!" shouted the people of Lower Train-switch, and jumped up from their hiding places. "Hurray for Tootle the Flyer!"

Now Tootle is a famous Two-Miles-a-Minute Flyer. The young locomotives listen to his advice.

"Work hard," he tells them. "Always remember to Stop for a Red Flag Waving. But most of all, Stay on the Rails No Matter What."